*For Eben, Jasper, Mia, Stella, Amelia, Miranda, Bridget, and Liam—*
*hugs to you all (but only if you want them) —C.F.*

*For the best huggers I know, Henry and Hugo —D.W.*

**G. P. PUTNAM'S SONS**
An imprint of Penguin Random House LLC, New York

Visit us online at penguinrandomhouse.com

Library of Congress Cataloging-in-Publication Data
Names: Finison, Carrie, author. | Wiseman, Daniel, illustrator.
Title: Don't hug Doug / by Carrie Finison; illustrated by Daniel Wiseman.
Other titles: Do not hug Doug
Description: New York: G. P. Putnam's Sons, [2021] | Summary: "Doug prefers not to be hugged,
but there are a variety of other ways his loved ones can show him affection"—Provided by publisher.
Identifiers: LCCN 2020012364 | ISBN 9781984813022 (hardcover) | ISBN 9781984813039 (ebook) |
ISBN 9781984813046 (kindle edition)
Subjects: CYAC: Hugging—Fiction. | Individuality—Fiction.
Classification: LCC PZ7.1.F5358 Don 2021 | DDC [E]—dc23
LC record available at https://lccn.loc.gov/2020012364

Manufactured in China by RR Donnelley Asia Printing Solutions Ltd.
ISBN 9781984813022
10   9   8   7   6   5   4   3   2

Design by Suki Boynton  •  Text set in Chalet Book  •  The art was done digitally.

# DON'T HUG DOUG

## (HE DOESN'T LIKE IT)

Thanks, but no thanks!

Written by **CARRIE FINISON**    Drawings by **DANIEL WISEMAN**

putnam

G. P. PUTNAM'S SONS

You can hug a pug.
(Awww!)

You can hug a bug.
(Maybe . . .)

You can hug a valentine. (Sweet!)

Or a porcupine. (Not recommended.)

Or a Frankenstein.

But don't hug Doug.

He doesn't like it.

Don't worry—Doug likes YOU.

He just doesn't like HUGS.

**Doug thinks hugs are:**

There are lots of things Doug *does* like.

He likes to sort his rock collection,

and try on his sock collection,

and draw with his chalk collection.

And he really likes harmonica bands.

Squeeeeak!

But he doesn't like hugs.

So, no matter how huggable he looks,
no matter how much you want to,
even if it's his birthday,
PLEASE don't hug Doug.

**What about hello hugs?**

**What about goodbye hugs?**

**What about game-winning home run hugs?**

**What about dropped ice cream cone hugs?**

There's only one kind
of hug Doug likes.
He likes a NOT squeezy,
NOT squashy,
NOT squooshy,
NOT smooshy,
JUST RIGHT
bedtime hug
from his mom.

Is it bedtime? Are you Doug's mom?

No, you're not. So . . . DON'T HUG DOUG!

Can you hug Doug's
pet potbellied pig?

**Ask!**

"Can we hug your pet potbellied pig?"

Some people love hugs.
Lots of people don't.
And lots of people are
somewhere in the middle.

So, can you hug Doug?
NO! He doesn't like it.

But he does like you!
And he likes high fives.

Doug is a master of high fives.

Straight five

Double five

Low five

Side five

Spinny five

Elbow five

He even has a high five for you.

Go ahead—ask!

"Hey, Doug! High five?"

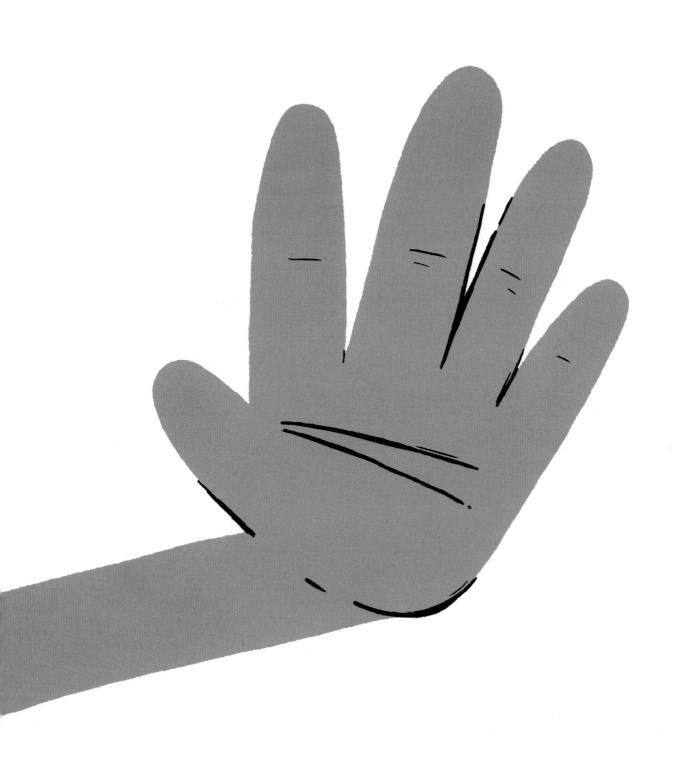